By Laurell K. Hamilton

(published by The Random House Publishing Group)

A KISS OF SHADOWS

A CARESS OF TWILIGHT

SEDUCED BY MOONLIGHT

A STROKE OF MIDNIGHT